Once Upon A Time series:

Cinderella

Concept and design:	Edward Glover
Typesetting:	Dave Organ
Production:	Johnson Lane
Audio recording:	Hat's Off
E-book production:	Innovations by Design Ltd

ISBN: 978-1-898250-22-7

Printed book: manufactured in China

10 9 8 7 6 5 4 3 2 1

E-book: produced in India and manufactured in China

Camelot Editions is a division of Transedition Limited
Oxford, England

Cinderella

Original story by Charles Perrault

Retold by Sally Byford

Illustrated by Eric Kincaid

CAMELOT EDITIONS

Once upon a time...

there was a girl who was beautiful, kind and gentle. When she was little, her mother died and her father married a proud and cruel woman with two spiteful daughters. As the years passed by, her father's work took him away from home and when he was gone, her stepmother made her do all the housework and dressed her in rags. Her stepsisters laughed at her and nicknamed her 'Cinderella' because she was always dirty from sweeping the cinders in the hearth. But Cinderella never lost hope. Every day, as she cooked and cleaned, she daydreamed of a happier life.

One day, Cinderella was scrubbing the scullery floor when she heard the sound of a trumpet outside the house and a loud rat-a-tat on the front door. She ran to see who it was, and there on the doorstep was a royal messenger. He gave a low bow and presented Cinderella with a large gold envelope with a red royal seal.

"Give it to me!" screamed her older stepsister, racing to the door. She snatched the envelope from Cinderella and ripped it open. "The King and Queen are holding a ball for the Prince to choose his bride," she cried. "And we've been invited!" The two stepsisters shrieked with excitement and danced around the room.

For the next few weeks, the two stepsisters talked of nothing but the ball. Their mother bought them the most expensive jewelry and hired the best dressmakers in the land. She was determined that one of her daughters would win the hand of the Prince.

"Can I go to the ball?" Cinderella dared to ask one day. Her stepmother glared at her. "It's impossible," she said coldly. "You have nothing to wear."

The night of the ball finally arrived. Cinderella ran around after her bossy stepsisters and stepmother, helping them to dress up in all their finery. "You've ruined my hair!" screamed the older stepsister. "You've brought me the wrong necklace," screeched the other.

When at last they left, they were bad-tempered and red-faced. Cinderella helped them into their carriage, and watched as they headed towards a wonderful evening of music and dancing.

For the first time, Cinderella's dreams began to fade and big wet tears rolled down her cheeks. She ran out into the garden, and wept beneath a willow tree.

"There's no need to cry, Cinderella," said a kind voice. "It isn't too late – you can still go to the ball." Cinderella looked up and there, in a haze of light, was a woman with bright, twinkling eyes. "I'm your fairy godmother, my dear," said the woman, "and I will make your wish come true."

"Can I really go to the ball?" gasped Cinderella.

Her fairy godmother smiled and nodded. "But first I need your help," she said. "Bring me a fine, fat pumpkin, one plump rat, six white mice and six slithery lizards. And be quick!"

Cinderella ran to the vegetable patch and chose a fine, fat pumpkin. She found a nest of six white mice in the roots of the apple tree, one plump rat in the potting shed, and six slithery lizards in the crevices of an old stone wall.

The fairy godmother murmured magical words and with a touch of her wand, the pumpkin was transformed into a glorious golden coach fit for a princess. The mice became six prancing white ponies, the rat was transformed into a fine, red-jacketed coachman, and the lizards turned into six slender footmen.

"Now your wish can come true," said the fairy godmother, as Cinderella span around with happiness.

Then Cinderella remembered her stepmother's
harsh words. "I can't go, fairy godmother,"
she said. "I have nothing to wear."

The fairy godmother just laughed and tapped
Cinderella on the shoulder with her wand.
In a flash, her rags and tatters were gone,
and Cinderella was dressed in the most
exquisite gown of shimmering silver.
On her feet were gleaming glass slippers
which perfectly fitted her dainty feet.

"Have a wonderful time," said her fairy godmother, as Cinderella waved from the coach. "But beware – the spell only lasts until midnight so you must leave before the clock strikes twelve."

"I won't forget," promised Cinderella, her eyes shining with excitement.

At the palace, Cinderella floated up a magnificent stairway and into a ballroom sparkling with chandeliers. All eyes turned towards the beautiful girl standing in the doorway, and voices whispered, "Who's she? I've never seen her before."

Cinderella gazed around the ballroom. The King and Queen were welcoming their guests, and the handsome Prince swirled a pretty partner across the dance floor. Cinderella spotted her stepsisters, still looking hot and cross. They were staring straight at her, but they didn't seem to recognise her at all.

Suddenly, the Prince bowed before Cinderella. "Would you like to dance?" he asked. Cinderella danced the next dance with the Prince, and the next and the next. Round and round they spun, the music singing in her ears, and the prince holding her tightly in his arms. Cinderella wished that the evening would last for ever.

"One, two, three," chimed the clock as midnight approached. But Cinderella didn't hear. She was too busy talking and laughing with the Prince. "Four, five, six," chimed the clock more loudly, and this time Cinderella did hear and her face grew pale.

"I've got to go!" she gasped, pushing through the crowds.

"Wait!" called the Prince. "Come back!" He tried to follow Cinderella through the ballroom, but as soon as the other ladies saw the Prince alone, they surrounded him, begging for a dance.

By the time the Prince reached the stairway, Cinderella was gone. All that was left of her was one glass slipper lying on the stairs.

The white ponies galloped as fast as they could until the clock struck midnight and the spell was broken. Then the pumpkin rolled to the side of the road, the mice, rat and lizards scampered away into the fields, and Cinderella had to walk the rest of the way home. She was dressed in her rags again, but her eyes still sparkled by the light of the moon.

The very next day, the Prince announced that he would search the kingdom high and low, until he found the lady who would fit the glass slipper.

There was great excitement when the Prince and his aide arrived at Cinderella's house and asked to see all the young ladies who lived there.

Cinderella's stepmother pushed her own two daughters forward. "Make sure one of you fits that slipper," she hissed.

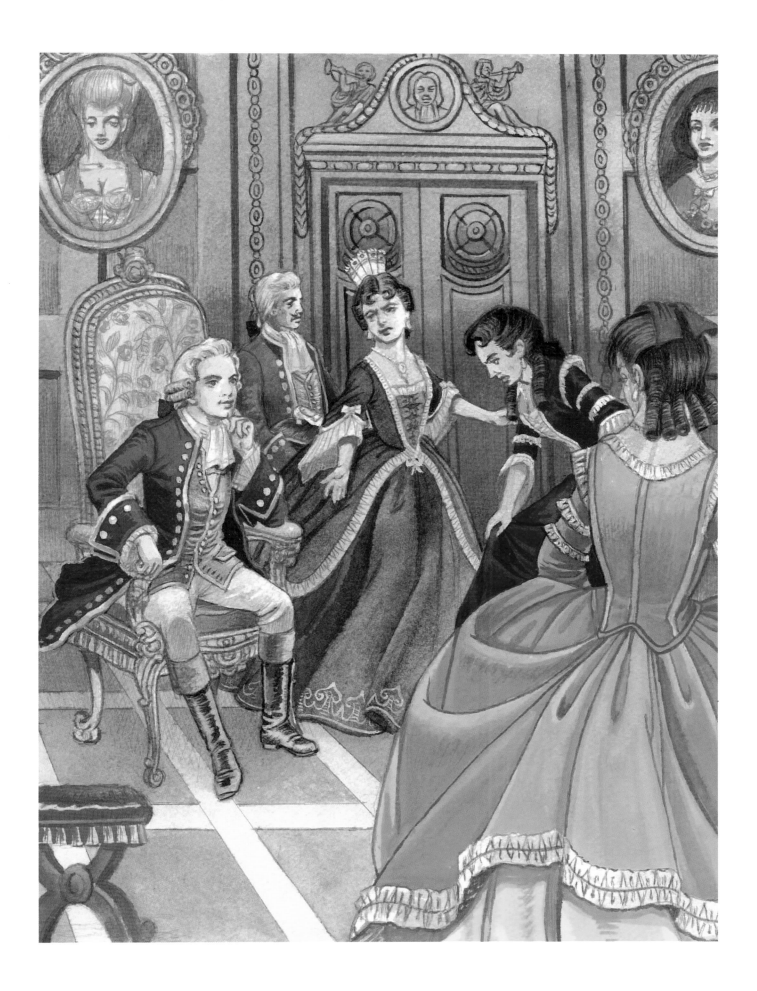

The older sister tried first. She squeezed her thin toes into the tiny slipper, but her foot was far too long.

The other sister stepped forward with a smug smile, for she knew her feet were smaller. But as she pushed her toes into the slipper, the smile left her face. Her foot was far too broad.

"What about this young lady?" asked the Prince, pointing to Cinderella who was cleaning out the fireplace.

At the Prince's invitation, Cinderella stepped forward with a curtsey and slipped her foot easily into the glass slipper. It was a perfect fit. Then Cinderella smiled up at the Prince, and when he saw her sparkling eyes, he knew at once she was his beautiful partner from the ball.

"This is ridiculous!" snapped her stepmother. "She didn't even go to the ball." She glared at Cinderella and grabbed her arm. "Get back to your work, girl. You're wasting the Prince's time." Then she gasped as Cinderella put her hand in her apron pocket and brought out the matching glass slipper.

The Prince was overjoyed he had found Cinderella and he asked her to marry him and become his princess. As he was as good and kind as he was handsome, Cinderella happily agreed. Everyone in the kingdom was invited to their wedding, even Cinderella's stepmother and stepsisters. The fairy godmother was the guest of honour, and Cinderella's father returned from his travels just in time for the celebrations.

Cinderella never had to cook or clean again, and she and the Prince lived happily ever after.